Meet ELLA

For Steven – RM

For Jade, whose first encounter with the
tooth fairy was not what she expected! – DM

Scholastic Australia
An imprint of Scholastic Australia Pty Limited (ABN 11 000 614 577)
PO Box 579 Gosford NSW 2250
www.scholastic.com.au

Part of the Scholastic Group
Sydney · Auckland · New York · Toronto · London · Mexico City
· New Delhi · Hong Kong · Buenos Aires · Puerto Rico

Published by Scholastic Australia in 2021.
Text copyright © Rebecca McRitchie, 2021.
Illustrations copyright © Danielle McDonald, 2021.

NATIONAL
LIBRARY
OF AUSTRALIA

A catalogue record for this
book is available from the
National Library of Australia

ISBN: 978-1-76097-392-6

The illustrations in this book were created digitally.
Typeset in KG Neatly Printed and Delius.
Design by Sofya Karmazina.

Printed in China by RR Donnelley.

Scholastic Australia's policy, in association with RR Donnelley, is to use papers that are
renewable and made efficiently from wood grown in responsibly managed forests, so as to
minimise its environmental footprint.

22 23 24 25 26 / 2

Meet ELLA

Tooth Trouble

REBECCA MCRITCHIE ❀ DANIELLE MCDONALD

A Scholastic Australia Book

CHAPTER ONE

Meet Ella. She is six years old. Ella likes **green apples** and the colour **blue**. Ella doesn't like holes in her socks or chewed pencils.

This morning, Ella is getting ready for school. She **brushes** her teeth with her blue stripey toothbrush. But as Ella brushes her teeth, something doesn't feel right.

Ella looks at her teeth in the mirror. They all look the same but when Ella touches her bottom tooth, it **wibbles** and **wobbles**.

Wow! Ella thinks. *My first loose tooth!*

'Ready for school photos?'
Dad asks.

Ella almost **forgot**. Today
is school photo day! Ella
runs back into the bathroom.
She puts a **blue bow** in her
hair. Now she is ready.

'Don't forget to do your **best smile**,' Dad says. He hands Ella her lunch bag.

'I hope I get to stand next to Zoe,' Ella says.

Ella and her **best friend** Zoe are almost the same height. The only person

taller than them in class is Alexander. And he is only taller by a little bit.

Mum drives Ella to school. Ella **practises** smiling her best smile.

CHAPTER TWO

In class, Ella sits next to Zoe. Zoe is wearing a **purple** headband. It is covered with stars that **sparkle**.

'I like your headband,' Ella says.

'Thanks,' says Zoe. 'I like your bow.'

'Nanna Kate gave it to me,' Ella says. 'She bought it from a **princess** in France.'

'Cool!' Zoe says.

'School photos will be after recess,' says Miss King. 'Meet me at the **school hall** as soon as the bell rings.'

At recess, Ella opens her lunch bag and finds a **green apple**. Her dad has packed her **favourite** fruit!

Ella bites into the juicy apple.
Then something happens.
Ella's bottom tooth wibbles
and wobbles. Then it **falls**
out right onto her hand!

'Is that your tooth?' Zoe
asks.

'Yes,' says Ella, but she
sounds different. A
whistle floats out from
the new gap in her teeth.

Ella covers her mouth with her hand.

Then the bell rings. It's the end of recess. The **school photos** are about to start.

'Oh no!' says Ella.

CHAPTER THREE

Ella and Zoe find Miss King. She is standing with the rest of Ella's **class** in the school hall.

'Look, Miss King,' Ella says with a **whistle**. She shows her teacher the tooth in her hand.

'Congratulations, Ella,' Miss King says. 'You've lost your first tooth.'

Miss King gives Ella a **small bag**. Ella puts her tooth inside it and zips it up.

'What about the photo?' Ella says. She looks at her tooth inside the bag.

'It's OK, Ella,' Miss King says. 'Everybody loses their teeth.'

'I think it looks **cool**,' says Zoe.

But Ella doesn't want a missing tooth. She doesn't want to whistle when she talks. She wants her **smile** back. Especially for school photo day.

'Take your places, girls. It's time for the **class photo**,' Miss King says.

Ella and Zoe stand in the back row next to Alexander.

He is **chewing** a pencil.

Ella tries to smile her best smile but she can't stop thinking about her missing tooth.

Ella sticks her tongue in
the gap between her teeth.
It feels funny.

Miss King says, 'Alright
class, say cheese. One,
two, **three!**'

'Cheese,' Ella says with a **whistle**. She hopes nobody hears it.

CHAPTER FOUR

At home, Ella tells her mum and dad what happened at school.

'That's **great**, Ella!' Dad says. He looks at Ella's tooth inside the bag.

'It's not great! It **ruined** the school photos. And I keep whistling,' Ella says with a whistle. 'See?'

'Your smile is still the best smile,' Mum says.

'I'm the only one in my **whole class** with a missing tooth,' Ella says.

It was true. Nobody else had lost their teeth yet. Not even Alexander.

'Everyone loses their baby teeth. Soon everyone else in your class will be whistling too,' Mum says.

'And the best thing about losing a tooth is the **tooth fairy**,' says Dad.

'The tooth fairy?' Ella asks.

'If you put your tooth under your **pillow** tonight, the tooth fairy will give you something **special** in return,' says Mum.

I wonder what she will give me, Ella thinks.

Later that night, Ella says goodnight to Mum and Dad and gives them a **cuddle**.

Before she goes to sleep, Ella places her tooth **under** her pillow.

Then she writes a little
note.

Dear Tooth Fairy,

Please take good
care of my tooth.

Love
Ella ♡

CHAPTER FIVE

In the morning, Ella jumps out of bed and looks under her pillow.

Ella's tooth is gone! And in its place is a shiny one dollar **coin**! The **tooth fairy** came!

'Wow!' Ella says. She can't **wait** to show Mum, Dad and Zoe!

At school, Zoe runs up to Ella.

'Ella, look what happened on the way to school this morning!' Zoe says happily.

She lifts up a bag in her hand. Sitting inside the clear bag is a small round **tooth**.

'See?' Zoe says, a **whistle** coming from her mouth.

Zoe smiles a **big smile** and Ella sees that she is missing one of her front teeth.

'Yay!' Ella says. She is no longer the only one with a tooth missing! Ella gives Zoe a **hug**.

'Now we're **matching**,'
says Zoe.

'Look what I got from the
tooth fairy this morning,'
Ella says.

Ella shows Zoe the **coin** and tells her all about the tooth fairy.

Zoe's eyes go wide. 'Cool!'
she says.

'Let's go to the **canteen**
at lunch and buy **icy poles**
with my coin,' Ella says.

Ella's dad was **right**. Losing your tooth is pretty **great**. In fact, Ella couldn't wait to lose another one.

If you loved  join her for more adventures!

And look out for more COMING SOON!